LINCOLN'S LEGACY

Read all the books
in the Blast to the Past® series!

#1 Lincoln's Legacy

#2 Disney's Dream

Coming soon:

#3 Bell's Breakthrough

By STACIA DEUTSCH
and RHODY COHON

LINCOLN'S LEGACY

Illustrated by DAVID WENZEL

Aladdin
New York London Toronto Sydney New Delhi

To our families, with love

Special thanks to: Alzada Tipton, Rona and Howard Perley, David Evenchick, Jonathan Anschell, Frank Weimann, and Jennifer Klonsky

ALADDIN
An imprint of Simon & Schuster Children's Publishing Division
1230 Avenue of the Americas, New York, NY 10020
This Aladdin paperback edition September 2013

Cover design by Jeanine Henderson

The text of this book was set in Minion Pro.
Manufactured in the United States of America 0813 OFF
2 4 6 8 10 9 7 5 3 1
Library of Congress Control Number 2004105709
ISBN 978-1-4424-9534-0
ISBN 978-1-4424-9871-6 (eBook)

Contents

1

Mondays

Every Monday, Mr. Caruthers came to class late.

Tuesday, Wednesday, Thursday, and Friday, he'd be waiting in the classroom before the bell rang. But never on Monday. There was something strange about Mondays.

And today was Monday.

When I entered the classroom, Maxine Wilson was already sitting at her table.

"Hey, Abigail," she greeted me. I always liked Maxine. We'd known each other since kindergarten.

"Are you ready?" I asked her.

"I'm always ready on Mondays." Maxine had a stopwatch.

The school bell was the signal.

Brrring.

Maxine pressed the little black button on her watch. “Go!” she shouted, and we all rushed to our seats.

Everyone sat silently, staring at the classroom door. No one dared look away. Not even for a second.

Maxine kept track of the time. “Four minutes, forty-nine seconds,” she announced.

The whole class always chanted the last ten seconds out loud together: “Ten. Nine. Eight. Seven. Six. Five. Four. Three. Two. One.” The door swung open.

“I’m sorry I’m late,” Mr. Caruthers apologized as he entered the classroom. We waited patiently while Mr. Caruthers straightened his crumpled suit jacket. Retied his bow tie. Combed his hair. And finally, pushed up his glasses.

Every Monday, Mr. Caruthers was late. Every Monday, he was wrinkled and messy. But it didn’t matter to us, the third-grade kids in classroom 305. Monday was our favorite day of the week. And Mr. Caruthers was our favorite teacher.

“Abigail,” Jacob whispered, leaning over to me.

“What do you think his question will be today?”

I shrugged and said softly, “I have no idea.”

Jacob turned to ask his brother Zack the same thing. Jacob and Zack were twins. They lived next door to me. And they were my table partners. Zack said he didn’t know either. A new kid named Roberto Rodriguez also sat at our table. But he didn’t talk much, so Jacob didn’t bother to ask him.

Mr. C finished straightening his clothes and leaned back on the edge of his desk. He was too cool to sit in a chair like other teachers.

“What if,” he began, and then paused. I sat up a little straighter. Every Monday, Mr. Caruthers asked us a new “what if” question. So far, my favorite questions were “What if Thomas Edison had quit and never invented the lightbulb?” and “What if Clara Barton had quit and never started the American Red Cross?”

I loved thinking up answers to Mr. C’s questions. And I couldn’t wait for this one.

Mr. C leaned back farther on his desk and finished his question. “What if Abraham Lincoln quit and never issued the Emancipation Proclamation?”

My hand shot up in the air. I didn't even wait for him to call on me. "What's the Emancipation Proclamation?" I blurted out. "Why's it so important?"

"Be patient, Abigail," Mr. Caruthers said slowly. "All your questions will be answered in good time."

"But—," I began. Mr. Caruthers looked at me over the top of his glasses. I put my hand down. It's really hard to wait when you are as curious as I am.

"Abraham Lincoln was the sixteenth president of the United States," Mr. Caruthers began. He told us that Abraham Lincoln was born in Kentucky in 1809. He was a lawyer. His wife's name was Mary Todd. And in 1860 he was elected president.

I really wanted to raise my hand again. He hadn't gotten to the Emancipation Proclamation part of the story yet. Struggling to keep quiet, I tucked my fingers under my legs and sat on them.

Mr. C continued telling Abraham Lincoln's story. "When Abraham Lincoln became president, there were only thirty-four states, not fifty like we have today. There were twenty-three states in the North, and eleven states in the South."

Mr. C pointed to Roberto. "Bo," Mr. C said, "do you have an idea?"

I turned my head to stare at the new kid. When I had something to say, Mr. C told me to wait. Why was he calling on a kid who hadn't even raised his hand? And since when was his name Bo? I guessed that was his nickname. I sure had a lot to learn about the new kid.

Bo spoke in a soft, small voice. "I read that on the very day Abraham Lincoln was elected president, the Southern states decided to start their own country. They called it the Confederate States of America and even elected Jefferson Davis to be their president. Is that right?" Bo sure knew a lot for such a quiet guy.

Mr. C slapped his hands together. "Yes, Bo. That's exactly what happened! The Southern states seceded from—or left—the United States. And a big war started."

"The Civil War?" Anna Ramos asked.

"Yes," Mr. C replied. "In the beginning, the war was about land. The North was fighting for all the states to stay one country. The South was fighting to have their own country with their own laws. But after the first year, slavery became the most important issue of the war."

It was so quiet in the classroom I could hear Cindy Cho biting her nails.

Mr. Caruthers explained, "Men, women, and children were brought from Africa to the Southern states. They were slave workers. They worked for no money and lived in horrible conditions. Very few ever escaped."

Even Cindy stopped biting her nails.

"African Americans who lived in the Northern states were already free. President Lincoln thought that all American people should be free." Mr. C pushed up his glasses. "Abraham Lincoln wanted to set the slaves free."

This was really interesting. But I still wanted to know about the Emancipation Proclamation. Finally Mr. C said the magic words:

"On September 22, 1862, President Lincoln issued the Emancipation Proclamation." Mr. C turned and wrote on the blackboard. "'Emancipation' means freedom," he told us. "And a 'proclamation' is an announcement." I eagerly copied his definitions in my notebook.

He wiped the chalk dust from his hands and faced the class. "The president ordered the Southern states to free their slaves. Since it was still the middle of the war, the Southern states ignored the Emancipation Proclamation. But when the North won the war, the South couldn't ignore it any longer. The slaves were set free." Mr. C folded his arms across his chest and sat back down on the edge of his desk.

"So today's question is: What if Abraham Lincoln quit and never issued the Emancipation Proclamation?" Mr. Caruthers gave us time to think about the answer.

He called on Danny Ochoa first. "I bet people fought harder knowing they were fighting for freedom," Danny suggested. "Without the Emancipation Proclamation, the North might have lost the war."

Anna Ramos said she thought that another leader might have freed the slaves instead.

Shanika Washington was worried that without the Emancipation Proclamation, her family might still be slaves. She wouldn't be allowed to go to school. She'd have to work for the person who owned her.

While the other kids were talking about the question, Zack leaned over to talk to his brother. They were talking so loudly, I couldn't help it. I had to listen.

"I don't get it," Zack said. "Why would Abraham Lincoln want to quit being president? If I were president of the United States, I'd never quit."

"Yes, you would," Jacob answered back. "You quit everything."

"Do not," Zack said, his voice rising.

Jacob reminded him to whisper. "Shhh. Remember chess club? The baseball team? Computer club?"

"Those don't count." Zack refused to whisper. "Besides, I still run track."

"Only because Mom and Dad make you." Now Jacob's voice was rising too.

"That's not true," Zack answered back. "I like

running." Zack's face was getting red. It was time for me to break things up.

I leaned over. "Cut it out. You guys are going to get us all in trouble."

It was too late. Mr. Caruthers was standing over my desk. He was so close I could actually count the wrinkles in his bow tie. "If you have something to say, I suggest you share it with the class."

I panicked. I wasn't going to tell my favorite teacher that I hadn't been paying attention. I desperately tried to think of something to say.

What would the world be like if Abraham Lincoln quit and never issued the Emancipation Proclamation? Anna, Danny, and Shanika had taken all the good answers.

Mr. Caruthers tapped his fingers on my desk.

"I—," I began. My mind was blank. "I just don't know." I sighed.

Mr. Caruthers didn't even blink. He calmly said, "I want to see you after school, Abigail." When Mr. Caruthers said my name, I thought he was kidding. I checked around to see if another Abigail had joined the class when I wasn't looking. There must have been some kind of mistake. I never got in trouble.

But Mr. Caruthers was looking straight at me. "After school, Abigail," he repeated.

2

Time Travel

After school I found Mr. Caruthers in the hallway in front of his classroom.

"I'm sorry," I said, lowering my eyes. I didn't want to look at him.

I held out a piece of lined, white notebook paper. I had written neatly on both sides. "I wrote an answer during recess," I explained.

Mr. Caruthers took the paper from me. "You didn't have to do extra work. Especially during recess."

"I wrote down what I thought would happen if Abraham Lincoln quit."

"Go ahead and tell me," he said. "I want to hear your idea."

"I thought about it all morning," I began. "If

Abraham Lincoln quit, the world would be a very different place. We would have two countries. There would be the United States of America and the Confederate States of America." I stopped and looked up at my teacher.

He looked around for a moment, then back at me. "Go on," Mr. Caruthers said.

"Without the Emancipation Proclamation, the two countries would be very different. Remember when you told us that there used to be big cities in the North and lots of farms in the South?" Mr. C nodded.

"Well," I continued, "I bet that nothing would change. In fact I think the North and South would each do their own thing. We would have two different kinds of money. Two different flags. There might even be a big wall separating the two countries."

I waited for Mr. Caruthers to say something. He didn't.

"The Southern states would still have slaves." I bit my lip. "And you might not be our teacher."

After a few seconds, Mr. Caruthers nodded. And pushed up his glasses. "Fine work, Abigail." He handed my paper back to me and abruptly looked down the hall.

"Oh, good," he said. "Here they come."

I looked where he was looking. Jacob and Zack were headed our way.

"Mr. C told us to meet him at the classroom after school," Jacob explained to me.

"But he didn't tell us why," Zack added. "Are we in trouble too?"

"No one is in trouble," Mr. Caruthers told us. "Come inside."

He was acting funny, like he had a big secret to share. We went into the classroom, but Mr. C stayed by the door. It was like he was waiting for one more person to join us. After another minute, Mr. C finally closed the door.

He went to his desk and sat in his chair. Mr. C motioned for us to move closer to him. When we were standing right next to him, he whispered, "It's not a game, you know."

"What isn't?" Jacob whispered back.

"'What if,'" Mr. C said. I could barely hear him, but I swear he said, "It's true."

I had no idea what Mr. Caruthers was talking about. "Do you mean, 'What if Abraham Lincoln quit and never issued the Emancipation Proclamation?'" I asked in my normal, loud voice.

"Shhh." Mr. Caruthers pressed his finger to his lips. He looked over at the classroom door. I think he was making sure no one had heard me. The door was still closed. No one could have heard anything.

"Yes," he whispered at last. "The questions I ask in class are real. Before school today, I went back to the year 1862 to convince Abraham Lincoln not to quit. He wouldn't listen to me."

Suddenly I noticed how red Mr. C's eyes were. He looked like he needed a nap.

"There was no way to force him to remain president. I couldn't issue the Emancipation Proclamation for him. I gave it my all, but he still quit." Mr. C took a deep breath and said, "I need you to help me convince him."

Zack rolled his eyes and made a crazy face. He thought Mr. Caruthers was telling us a funny joke. Or playing a trick. "Why do you need us?" he asked with a silly grin. "We're just kids. We aren't even the smartest kids in class."

Zack had a good point. I wasn't the smartest, but I sure tried the hardest. Jacob wasn't the smartest either, unless you counted everything he knew about computers.

Mr. Caruthers looked at each of us for a long moment, then explained. "You are each special. And together you make a great team."

"We sound like superheroes." Zack laughed.

"It's not a joke, Zack," Mr. Caruthers said seriously. He reached into his coat pocket and pulled out a handheld video game. It looked different from any game I'd ever seen before. There were four extra buttons and a bigger screen. I looked more closely. It wasn't a game. It was a computer.

Mr. Caruthers took a square cartridge out of his pocket. It had a picture of Abraham Lincoln on it.

"When you put this into the back of the computer,

it will take you to September 22, 1862. The day Abraham Lincoln issued the Emancipation Proclamation. After you convince him not to quit, take out the cartridge," Mr. Caruthers explained. "The computer is programmed to bring you back to school."

He handed Jacob the computer and cartridge.

"Wow!" Jacob exclaimed. His eyes lit up and sparkled with excitement. "What are these buttons for?" Jacob asked about the four little red buttons below the computer's screen.

"Those buttons let you make changes in the computer's settings," Mr. C explained. "If you press the buttons, you can pick other places to visit. Or other times." Mr. Caruthers wrinkled his nose. "You better get going." He handed Jacob his wristwatch. "Keep track of your time. The cartridge only lasts two hours."

"That's perfect," I said. "I have to be home at the end of club time."

"But is two hours long enough?" Jacob asked as he put on Mr. Caruthers's watch. It was too big and slipped off his hand. He tightened it.

"It has to be," Mr. Caruthers said. "I can't get you

any extra time. There are a few flaws in the computer's design." Mr. Caruthers sighed loudly. "You have only two hours." Then I heard him say under his breath, "There's also that awful explosion."

"Explosion?" I asked, getting a little nervous.

"Never mind." He shook his head. "The important thing is that you kids get to use a brand-new cartridge. Unfortunately, I had no success this morning and used up my whole cartridge trying. Abraham Lincoln must issue the Emancipation Proclamation and free the Southern slaves on September 22, 1862. If he doesn't, when we wake up tomorrow, our world might be very different." He pointed at the essay in my hand. "Good luck."

Then our teacher left the classroom.

Jacob turned the computer around in his hand, examining it. "Where do you think he got this thing?" he asked me.

"At the mall," Zack answered.

"I don't think he was joking, Zack." I didn't have time to say anything else because the classroom door swung open.

It was Bo, the new kid. "I forgot my backpack." He was looking down, shuffling his feet and talking so softly I could barely hear him. "Mr. Caruthers told me to come get it after school. He didn't tell me anyone else would be here."

Jacob tried to hide the computer behind his back. But Bo had already seen it.

"What's that?" he mumbled.

"It's nothing!" Jacob and I shouted at the same time. Mr. Caruthers hadn't told us not to show the computer to anyone else. But we were pretty sure it was a secret.

"Whatever," Bo muttered, picking up his backpack to leave.

Just then, Jacob accidentally dropped the cartridge. It slid next to Bo's feet.

Bo picked it up. "Here." Bo opened his hand. Jacob held out the machine and, without thinking, let Bo slip the cartridge into the back slot.

Suddenly a huge hole appeared in the floor, right next to Mr. Caruthers's desk. A big green glowing hole with smoke coming out of it.

"Whoa. That's a deep hole," Bo said. He took a little step forward to check it out, but his foot got tangled in his backpack strap and he tripped. He fell into the hole and disappeared.

Zack looked at the empty place where Bo had just been standing. "I'm out of here," Zack said. "I forgot to feed the dog."

Jacob blocked his way to the door. "We don't have a dog."

"That's right. I forgot to go to the pet store and get a dog." Now Zack knew for sure that Mr. Caruthers wasn't joking. He was scared.

The green hole was shrinking.

I was scared too, but we had no choice. I put my essay down on Mr. C's desk.

"We have to go get Bo," I said, stepping forward. My heart was pounding hard. I closed my eyes and imagined I was at the swimming pool on the diving board.

"Are you coming?" I asked Jacob and Zack.

"I'm coming." Jacob stepped next to me and took my hand.

“You aren’t leaving me here.” Zack held my other hand.

“What about the dog?” I asked.

“I’ll get one tomorrow.” He smiled.

“Let’s go!” I shouted, and together we jumped.

3

Washington

We definitely weren't at school anymore. The air was cool and it was raining a little. I shivered. My feet were freezing.

"Oh, man," I said, looking down at my new tennis shoes. I was standing in a very muddy puddle. I bent my knees and jumped out of the mud. I landed in a pile of trash.

"Oh, man," I said again, looking down at my shoes. "I should have worn boots." The whole street was made of dirt and mud and little pools of greenish goopy water. And where there wasn't mud there was garbage.

"Are you sure we're in the right place?" I asked Jacob.

Jacob checked the computer. He shook it and

pressed a button. "The computer seems to be working all right," he said. Then he looked around and added, "Maybe there are a few other glitches that Mr. C didn't mention?"

"Like maybe it doesn't work?" Zack said. "Let's find Bo and get out of here."

Suddenly Zack plugged his nose and said loudly, "Pe-ew! What is that smell?"

"It's not me," Jacob said. "I showered this morning."

I started to say, "It's not me, either," when Zack tapped me on the shoulder. He could barely speak. "Look," he breathed. Hundreds, maybe even thousands, of brown cows were headed toward us.

"Is this a city or a farm?" Jacob moaned. He grabbed Zack by the arm. The cows were getting closer. And they were coming fast. There was no time to look for Bo. We had to run.

We took off down the street. But the cows were after us. A big cow stuck her nose in my back, and I stumbled forward. Jacob caught me and pulled me away before I was trampled.

"This way!" Zack led us toward a small patch of

grass at the end of the street. We ran through the mud, jumping over puddles as best we could. Zack is the fastest runner I know. But even he was slowed down by the muddy goop.

We were near the grass when suddenly a boy's voice called out to us. It was hard to hear what he was saying. The cows were very noisy. Then we heard it again. He was yelling, "Over here!" We ran toward the voice.

It was Bo. He was standing in the doorway of a small wooden shed. We ran inside and slammed the door shut.

The shed turned out to be a stable. There was hay all over the floor. But luckily, no horse. I could hear the cows passing by outside.

"Thanks, Bo," I said. "Good thing you found us." I wondered what Mr. C would say when he found out Bo had time-traveled with us—and had saved us from a huge herd of cows.

"I'm glad you found me, too," Bo said. I was surprised at how loudly he spoke. I'd never heard him talk in more than a whisper before. "When the cows came," Bo said, nervously biting his bottom lip, "I ran into this shed. I've never seen so many cows in my life. I didn't know what else to do."

I told Bo I had never seen so many cows either. None of us knew why they were in the city.

"I found this." Bo picked up a newspaper off the hay. "And I read it. It doesn't say anything about the cows. But I did learn that we are in Washington, D.C. And that it is September 22, 1862." He put the paper back down. "I just can't figure out how we got here or how we get back home."

Jacob told Bo about the handheld computer and the Abraham Lincoln cartridge.

Bo scratched his chin. "So, we only have two hours to convince Abraham Lincoln that he shouldn't quit being president of the United States?" he asked.

"And, most important, he has to issue the Emancipation Proclamation," I added.

Jacob put the computer in his pocket. He checked his watch. "Actually," he said, "now we have only one hour and forty minutes." A cow snorted loudly outside the shed.

"We better get started," I said. "I think we need a plan."

Jacob peeked his head out the door. "If we are here to find Abraham Lincoln, let's find him." Jacob found an opening between two cows and disappeared into the sea of cattle.

"Yeah," Zack mumbled. "Then maybe we can go home." Zack followed Jacob out of the stable.

"So much for a plan," I sighed. Bo and I rushed to catch up with them.

At the corner, the cows turned right. So we went left.

This new street was different. It was less muddy because there were large rocks stuck to the ground. But even without the mud and the cows, it was still hard to move around. Men in blue army uniforms were everywhere. It was very crowded.

And it was noisy. There was a marching band in front of us. Another band was coming up behind us. A trumpet tooted loudly in my ear.

We'd stepped into the middle of a parade.

We moved slowly through the crowd, trying to stay together.

"We're wasting time," I shouted into Jacob's ear. "Where are we going?"

"To see the president," he shouted back at me. He pointed up at a street sign. It read PENNSYLVANIA AVENUE. I knew that the White House was on Pennsylvania Avenue.

"Good idea, Jacob," I hollered. "But where is the White House?"

"I don't know," he screamed. We stopped to look around. It was hard to see very far with the crowds. Plus there were three hot air balloons blocking our view of the sky.

"It has to be around here somewhere," Bo yelled.

A newspaper boy was standing on the corner. I tugged on Jacob's shirt. "Maybe we can ask him directions," I shouted. Jacob nodded.

The paperboy was wearing pants that tied around his knees and a funny flat hat. He was waving a newspaper and shouting the headline, "'The Great Gorilla Is a Coward!'"

Then he picked up a different newspaper and

PENNSYLVANIA

called out, "'The Slangwhanging Stump Speaker Is Shattered!'"

We worked our way through the crowd to the newspaper boy. Instead of asking for directions, Zack asked, "Who are you shouting about?"

"Abraham Lincoln, of course," the paperboy answered.

Zack turned to his brother. "There must be two Abraham Lincolns. He can't be talking about President Lincoln. Everybody loves President Lincoln. He freed the slaves."

"He hasn't freed them yet," Jacob reminded his brother. "That's why we're here."

The newspaper boy interrupted us. "Do you want to buy a paper? I have a few more headlines. You can have one that says: 'The Mole-Eyed Monster Is Unfit to Lead.' Or: 'The Original Baboon Must Resign!' Which one do you want?"

"When I was in the stable I read the article about the Mole-Eyed Monster." Bo shook his head. "It wasn't very nice."

Suddenly I understood. And by the look in Zack's eyes, he got it too.

There was only one Abraham Lincoln. Some newspapers were making fun of him because he was too tall and had really long arms. Other papers said he looked like a monster because he was skinny and had a big nose. But no matter how they said it, all the newspaper headlines had the same message: Abraham Lincoln should quit.

We had to find him. Quickly.

"Which way to the White House?" I asked the newspaper boy.

"Never heard of it," the boy answered.

How could he never have heard of the White House? We were standing on Pennsylvania Avenue! I asked the same question a different way. "We are looking for the big house with the Oval Office and the Rose Garden. It is surrounded by a big fence. And protected by Secret Service agents."

"Never heard of it," the boy repeated. He turned away to sell a soldier a paper.

Bo scratched his chin. He was thinking hard. "None of those things existed in 1862. President Taft built the Oval Office in 1909. Woodrow Wilson's wife, Ellen, planted the Rose Garden in 1913. And Abraham Lincoln himself created the Secret Service in 1865."

"Wow," I said to Bo. "How do you know all that?" I was amazed at how much he already knew about President Lincoln and the White House.

"I like to read." Bo shrugged. "I read a lot."

"Good thing we brought you along." Jacob laughed.

"Good thing I'm clumsy." Bo smiled, remembering how he tripped and fell into the green hole.

I was starting to like Bo. He was talking a little more now that we were getting to know each other better. Maybe we could be friends after all.

"So, if it isn't called the White House," I asked, "how are we going to find it?"

"Too easy." Jacob winked. "What does every White House have in common?"

I thought about it a second. So did Zack. And Bo.

"Presidents!" We all shouted at the same time. I

turned back to the newspaper boy. "Where does President Lincoln live?" I asked.

"The President's Palace," the boy answered. "But he calls it the Executive Mansion." He grabbed a paper off a pile. "Are you going to buy a newspaper or not?" He shook the paper in my face.

I blinked hard. We needed a president. Not a paper. One last question and we'd go away. "Where's the President's Palace?" I asked quickly.

"Your eyes ain't worth a goober!" The boy pointed straight ahead and up a hill.

I wasn't sure what he meant. But it didn't sound like a compliment.

We moved away from the crowd to get a better look. And there it was! We hadn't seen it before because of the crowd and the hot air balloons.

"Cool!" Jacob said. "It looks almost exactly like the White House in our time." I waved thank you to the paperboy. He ignored me.

"What if Abraham Lincoln isn't home?" Zack asked. I stared at him for a second.

Then we took off running.

④

Looking for Lincoln

There was no fence around the White House. Bo had already told us that the Secret Service didn't exist in 1862, so there was no one guarding the door. It was weird to just walk right into the White House. It was even stranger that a woman in a yellow dress and matching hat held the door open for us.

No one was going to stop us.

We were standing in the entry hall. There was a long hallway and two staircases.

"Which way?" I asked Bo. I hoped Bo knew enough about the White House to help us find President Lincoln.

"I've read about American presidents. I've even visited Washington, D.C.," Bo said with a shrug. "But

I've never actually been inside the White House."

"May I help you?" A young man in a long black coat came up beside us. He told us that he was the president's secretary.

"We're looking for President Lincoln," I said, still surprised that we'd just walked right into the White House. "Do you know where he is?"

"Well," he said, "I would not go that way." He pointed downstairs. "The Executive Mansion was built on swampland. The basement stinks." Then he added, "The president's office is upstairs."

We quickly thanked him and rushed up the stairs two at a time. We had to find President Lincoln. America needed him to issue the Emancipation Proclamation.

"Over here." Jacob found an open door. We went inside.

"This can't be the president's office," I said. On the far side of the room was a small stage covered with a thick velvet curtain. A basket of puppets sat on the floor.

Zack picked up a marionette. "Forget Lincoln. Let's do a show instead." He made the puppet dance.

"No way." Jacob checked the watch. "We don't have time."

We split up. I checked the room next door. And the room next to that one. And three other rooms, too. There was no sign of President Lincoln. In fact there was no sign of anyone.

"This place is huge," I complained when I ran into Bo in the hallway. He hadn't found the president either.

"Until the end of the Civil War, the White House was the biggest building in America," Bo explained.

We checked two more rooms together. No sign of President Lincoln.

Suddenly Jacob called, "Come here quick!"

Bo and I practically flew down the hall. Zack was already there.

We were in a green room. The wallpaper was green. The carpets were green too. Civil War maps were tacked to the walls. And newspapers were spread on the desk. More newspapers were lying on a side table. And even more newspapers had been tossed in two baskets on the floor.

"Way to go, Jacob!" I did a little happy dance. "This must be Abraham Lincoln's office. But where's the president?"

A man came into the room. He wore a dark suit with a shirt that buttoned all the way up to his neck.

"Wow! That's William Seward," Bo whispered to me. "I have a biography about him at home. He looks just like he does in the pictures. He wanted to be president but ended up being the secretary of state instead."

"Excuse me, Mr. Seward," I said. "Have you seen President Lincoln?"

"I was just coming to look for him." William Seward seemed nice at first, but then his face turned angry. "Wait a minute. How do you know who I am?" William Seward asked with a growl. "And what are you doing in the Executive Mansion?"

"We have to talk to the president," Jacob told him. "And we don't have much time."

William Seward stared at us for a long moment. "Spies!" he suddenly shouted. "I found spies!" He grabbed Bo by the neck of his shirt. "Do you know what we do to spies?"

Bo's face went white. He mouthed the word, "Prison."

"Prison!" Zack choked. "Let's get out of here!" He stared at the pocket where Jacob had stashed the time-travel machine.

But before Jacob could get the computer, William Seward grabbed him by the arm. With one hand holding Bo and the other on Jacob, he dragged the two boys into the next room. Zack and I had no choice. We had to stick with our friends. So we followed.

"I captured four Confederate spies!" William Seward shoved the boys toward a back corner. He grabbed my shoulder and Zack's arm and pushed us into the same corner. "I caught them snooping in the president's office."

The four of us scooted back against the wall, as far away from William Seward as we could.

"Oh," Bo gasped, looking around. "These men are all in that book I told you about." He tilted his head

toward a man sitting by the window. "That's Salmon Chase, the secretary of the treasury." He put his hand to his chin and held it there. "And that's Edwin Stanton. He's the secretary of war." Mr. Stanton had a bushy mustache and a long beard.

Bo told us the names of all the men in the room. "These are the men who give Abraham Lincoln advice," he explained. "This is his executive cabinet." He was amazed.

"And they are going to send us to prison," Zack reminded us. "We should get out of here." He told Jacob to get the computer and pull out the cartridge.

"They can't send us to prison, because we aren't spies." Jacob stubbornly shoved the computer down deeper in his pocket. "We aren't leaving until we see the president!"

Edwin Stanton squinted his eyes at us. He looked at each of us slowly and carefully. He made up his mind and declared, "These children aren't spies." He told William Seward to let us go.

"Yes, they are," William Seward argued. He pointed right at me. "Just look at their strange disguises."

All the men at the table began whispering and pointing at our clothing.

I was wearing my favorite blue jeans and a new shirt. Bo and Jacob were wearing T-shirts and shorts. Zack had on a T-shirt and pants with a hole in the knee.

There was nothing strange about our clothes.

"I will agree they look mighty strange. But that does not mean they are spies," Edwin Stanton argued. "If I were president, these children would never have gotten into the Executive Mansion in the first place," he announced.

Bo leaned over to me and said softly, "Edwin Stanton wants to be president of the United States too."

"Is there anyone who doesn't want to be president?" I whispered back.

"Yeah," Bo answered. "Abraham Lincoln."

"Oh, right," I said. "What should we do?" Bo didn't have any good ideas.

William Seward stared at us long and hard. Then he said to the cabinet members, "We live in a democracy. Let us vote. Are they spies or not?"

I crossed my fingers and hoped we wouldn't go to prison.

"Not," Edwin Stanton said. One by one, the other men agreed.

And it was decided. We weren't spies. I uncrossed my fingers and started breathing again.

William Seward nodded. "It has been decided," he announced. "You must leave the Executive Mansion immediately," he said. "You have interrupted a very important meeting. If there is good news about the war, President Lincoln is going to issue a proclamation."

"The war is not going well. And I bet my teeth he is not coming," Edwin Stanton said angrily. He called the president a few mean names. He really didn't like President Lincoln at all.

"Let us go home. Maybe there will be better news tomorrow," Salmon Chase suggested.

"Good idea," Zack heartily agreed. He headed to the door.

"No one can go home!" Jacob countered, blocking

Zack's way. Then he announced, "We're going to get President Lincoln."

"We are?" I asked.

"Yes," Jacob told me. "We've got to get him. It's the only way."

"But he is not in the Executive Mansion," Salmon Chase complained.

"He does not come to receptions or teas or important meetings," Gideon Welles, secretary of the navy, added.

"President Lincoln is at the War Department," Edwin Stanton explained. "He watches the telegraph machine and waits for news of the war." He paused. "He stays there all day and night."

"We'll go find President Lincoln." I tried to sound confident. "We'll have him here before your meeting is over."

William Seward said, "Tell the president he must be here within the hour. We will not wait a minute longer."

Jacob checked the time on Mr. C's watch. "Perfect. We have exactly one hour before our time runs out."

As we left the meeting room, I turned to Bo. "Which way to the War Department?"

Bo hurried back to President Lincoln's office to look at one of the maps on the wall. When he returned, he knew where to go.

"Great," I said. "Let's get Lincoln!"

5

Abraham Lincoln

The rain was still falling, but this time the mud didn't slow us down. We knew where we were going. And exactly what we had to do.

The War Department was also on Pennsylvania Avenue, only a short way from the White House. We ran past two marching bands and hundreds of soldiers. There weren't hot air balloons in the sky anymore. I figured they all landed because of the rain.

We found the columned entrance to the building easily. And found the telegraph room even more easily. We just followed the clicking noise of the telegraph machine.

I knew from class that telegraphs were used before telephones were invented. They were a way for people to send messages over a wire. Telegraphs were quicker than the mail, but still slow. If there wasn't a telegraph office nearby, you had to go find one. President Lincoln was at the War Department because the White House didn't have a telegraph office.

We went inside expecting to see Abraham Lincoln sitting next to the telegraph machine, reading the news of the war. But instead a young man was standing by the telegraph, translating the coded messages.

I started to ask where we could find the president when Zack called out, "He's back here."

A man was sitting against the wall in the darkest corner of the room. He had his head tucked into his knees so I couldn't see his face. But I'd have recognized him anywhere.

"President Lincoln?" I said. I wasn't sure how to talk to the president of the United States. "Sir?"

He looked up and stroked his beard with one hand. "Ah, yes. There you are." He rose off the floor and straightened to his full height. I knew he was a tall man. But he was much taller than I had imagined.

"I've been waiting for you," he said. He walked over to a small desk and sat down.

"You have?" Jacob asked. Jacob looked at me. I looked at Bo. Bo looked at Zack. We were really confused.

"Take this letter to the Executive Mansion." He tucked a piece of paper into an envelope. "My cabinet is meeting on the second floor. Deliver it to the men assembled."

President Lincoln thought we were messengers. He handed Jacob the envelope.

"What's in it?" I asked. "Is it the Emancipation Proclamation? Are you going to free the slaves?"

"This letter is much more important than any proclamation," he replied. Then after a short pause he said, "That reminds me of a joke—" He stopped suddenly. "I mean—" He paused again and said softly, "I love jokes, but I cannot tell jokes today."

"Why not?" Zack asked. "I'm always in the mood for a joke."

"I am not in the mood for humor." Abraham Lincoln looked down at his feet. "I feel too sad.

We are fighting a war we cannot possibly win."

"But the North *will* win the war," I said strongly.

Abraham Lincoln wasn't listening to me.

A worker came and handed him a telegraph message. President Lincoln didn't even look at it. He just dropped it on the floor.

"I cannot bear to read it," he said sadly. "It will just be news of another bloody battle. One more terrible defeat for my troops." He paused. "I want to free the slaves, but my army can't seem to win anywhere. I wrote the Emancipation Proclamation two months ago and have been waiting for a victory. All I need is one. I cannot issue the Emancipation Proclamation if we are losing the war."

"I get it," Zack said. "Winners never take orders from losers."

"I suppose that is one way to say it," Abraham Lincoln replied.

"But you won't be the loser," I said. "The North is going to win and the states will be one country again. You will be everyone's president. And you will free the slaves." I was trying very hard to convince him.

President Lincoln stared at me. "Winning the war is a dream," he said. "A silly dream. The North cannot win the war. And I cannot free the slaves." He shook his head.

President Lincoln pointed to the letter in Jacob's hand. "You have been hired as messengers. Go now. Deliver my letter of resignation." He walked back to the dark corner of the office and sank back down onto the floor.

"Wait!" I said. "You can't resign!"

He looked at me long and hard. "I must do what is right for my country." President Lincoln drew up his knees to his chest.

"I quit!" he declared.

Then he lowered his head to his knees and sighed.

⑥

The Future

I looked over at Bo. He was scratching his chin, thinking hard. "We need a plan," he said.

"Duh." I smacked myself on the forehead.

"I thought we had one," Jacob replied. "We were going to take President Lincoln back to the White House so he can issue the Emancipation Proclamation."

"Forget it." Zack rolled his eyes to the ceiling. "We tried our best. President Lincoln doesn't want to go back to the Executive Mansion. He doesn't want to issue the Emancipation Proclamation. If he wants to quit, maybe we should just let him."

"We can't let him quit." I punched Zack in the arm.

Zack rubbed his arm. "If Mr. C couldn't convince

him, how can we?" He grabbed a small gold-colored bowl off a nearby table. "We'd have a better chance hitting him over the head, knocking him out, and dragging him to the White House."

"He's too big for us to carry." Jacob took the bowl from Zack and put it back on the table. "So we are going to have to try harder to convince him."

We hadn't left the telegraph office, but Abraham Lincoln didn't seem to notice. In fact we were standing right next to him, but he wasn't looking at us. He was still sitting on the floor with his head resting on his knees.

"I already told him the North would win the war," I said. "He didn't listen."

"He didn't believe you," Bo confirmed. "All he knows is that the North is losing."

"I'll go tell him we are from the future. Maybe that will work," Jacob suggested. Jacob took the computer out of his pocket and went over to the president.

"President Lincoln," he began. "We aren't your messengers. We're from the future." Jacob showed him the computer. "We came to tell you that you must issue the Emancipation Proclamation today. You can't quit."

President Lincoln stood up once again. He towered over Jacob. "So you come from the future?" Jacob nodded. "Well, I told you I love jokes. This is a really good one," President Lincoln said. He tried to laugh, but squeaked instead. He sighed. "I feel too sad to laugh." He didn't even look at the computer. "Go." President Lincoln pointed at the exit. "Deliver my letter."

Jacob sighed and stepped back. "This is going to be harder than I thought," he groaned.

I'd tried my best to convince President Lincoln. Jacob had tried.

Now it was Bo's turn.

I could tell Bo loved being around all these famous Americans. But I could also tell he didn't really want to talk to them. It took all his courage. Bo took a big step forward and looked up at President Lincoln. Way up.

"Are you still here?" Abraham Lincoln asked. "You are the worst messengers I have ever met. What will it take to get you to leave?" President Lincoln reached into his pocket. He took out a few coins and handed them to Bo. "You have been paid. Now go!"

I thought Bo might turn and run away. But he took a deep breath and said, "Five days ago, the Northern army won a battle at Antietam. It wasn't a great victory. But it was good enough." Bo tapped his foot nervously and said softly, "Now will you issue the Emancipation Proclamation?"

"We didn't win at Antietam," President Lincoln told Bo. "In fact Antietam is turning out to be the biggest disaster of them all. So far, more troops have been lost at Antietam than in any other battle of the Civil War."

President Lincoln went to his desk. He opened the drawer and took out a stack of telegrams. He showed Bo the telegrams.

"We lost at Thoroughfare Gap. We lost at Richmond and Harpers Ferry. We almost won at Chantilly, but no one really won that one." Then he picked up the telegram he had thrown on the floor when we first met him. He read it quickly and said, "And we are losing at Antietam."

"No," Bo challenged. "The North wins. After that, General McClellan messes up. He doesn't chase after the Southern troops. He just lets them leave. It's a mistake, but all the history books say the same thing." Bo put his hands on his hips and rose up on his tiptoes. He looked up at Abraham Lincoln and said, "I know it for a fact. The North wins at Antietam."

It was so unlike Bo, I nearly laughed. I couldn't believe my eyes. Bo was talking loudly to President Abraham Lincoln. Bo was telling President Lincoln he was wrong.

President Lincoln handed Bo the telegram about Antietam. "We are losing the war."

Bo scanned the telegram. Then he handed it back to President Lincoln. Without another word, Bo slowly turned and walked away.

He came to where we were waiting. "I tried," Bo muttered. The old Bo was back. He was speaking so softly, I could barely hear him. "I don't get it. I know for sure that on September seventeenth, the North won at Antietam. Why doesn't he know about the victory?"

"I don't know," I sighed. We were running out of ideas. And out of time.

Then I realized there was one last thing we hadn't tried.

"Anybody have a penny?" I asked. Only the best presidents get their pictures on money. And he was one of the best. Maybe a penny would convince him not to quit.

We all emptied our pockets. Bo had the coins Abraham Lincoln had given him. Zack had a paper-clip and a gum wrapper. I had some lint. And Jacob pulled out the computer. No one had pennies.

Suddenly Zack started punching the air. "Abigail just gave me a great idea." He was so excited he could barely speak. "Give me the computer."

"No way," Jacob argued. "You're going to send us home."

"No, I'm not." They locked eyes. Zack blinked first. "Fine," he groaned, "I'll just tell you my idea instead."

The twins put their heads together. Zack whispered. Jacob nodded. Suddenly Jacob jumped and shouted, "Awesome idea! You shouldn't have quit computer club!" Jacob fiddled with the buttons on the front of the computer. The machine beeped loudly.

"What are you guys doing?" Bo asked.

"Abraham Lincoln wants us to leave, so we're going to leave," Jacob answered. He pushed a few more buttons. The computer beeped again.

"Only we are taking him with us," Zack added.

Jacob explained. "Putting the cartridge in the computer brought us here. Taking it out will send us back. Mr. C said that if we press these special red buttons we can change our landing place. So instead of going to school, we're going to Washington, D.C."

"*Our* Washington, D.C." Zack gave his brother a high five.

Jacob pulled the cartridge out of the back of the handheld computer. A big, deep, glowing green hole appeared in the dark corner of the telegraph office.

"What the dickens is going on?" President Lincoln stomped over to the corner. He stepped to the edge of the hole to get a better look. Zack leaped up and grabbed the president around the waist. The two of them tumbled into the swirling mist together. Jacob jumped in after them.

"Do you think we have a chance?" I asked Bo. "Can we convince him to issue the Emancipation Proclamation?"

"I hope so. At least now we have a plan." Bo took my hand in his. "Hang on tight."

On the count of three we jumped.

And on the count of four we landed, because time travel is really fast.

7

Washington, D.C.

"Help!" It was Zack. "He's squashing me!"

"Oh, no," I said, looking down at the sidewalk. Abraham Lincoln had Zack pinned to the ground.

"Oops. I guess I should have warned Zack." Bo shrugged. "Abraham Lincoln's favorite sport is wrestling."

Abraham Lincoln held tightly to Zack. "Where are we?" he demanded to know. "What have you done to me? Where is the telegraph office?" His face was red. He was really mad. "Where is the city of Washington?"

Jacob was laughing so hard his eyes were watering. I moved in to try to help Zack, but Jacob

grabbed my arm and held me back. "Zack doesn't really need help," he told me. "Just watch."

Zack was surprisingly calm when he told President Lincoln, "This is Washington, D.C., in the future." I watched Zack wiggle his right arm free. "We brought you to the Lincoln Memorial." Somehow Zack got his left leg free. "Abigail gave me the idea. Your face is on the front of every penny. And this building is on the back." Then in an amazing wrestling move, Zack flipped Abraham Lincoln onto the sidewalk.

"I knew he could do it," Jacob said proudly as Zack stood up. "He was on the wrestling team for a whole week."

Abraham Lincoln stood up too. He dusted off his black suit and said very seriously, "There is no such thing as time tra . . ." His voice trailed off.

A car whizzed by. Abraham Lincoln watched it pass. He gave Jacob a questioning look. "That's called an automobile," Jacob told him. Abraham Lincoln repeated the word. Jacob showed him the streetlights. A boy on a skateboard. Then an airplane in the sky.

"In our time, people can travel through the air,"

Jacob began to explain, but Zack cut him off.

"He isn't here to learn about the Wright brothers," Zack interrupted. "We have to tell him why the Emancipation Proclamation is so important."

"I'm getting to that part," Jacob argued.

"Time's running out." Zack grabbed Jacob's wrist and looked at his watch. "Forty-two minutes left," he reported. "Talk faster."

While we were talking, Abraham Lincoln was already halfway to the top of the steps of the Lincoln Memorial building.

We rushed to catch up.

Before we reached the top step, President Lincoln raised a finger to his lips. "Listen!" he commanded in his presidential tone.

We stopped. We heard a woman's voice. She spoke loudly, clearly. And for a second, none of us moved. We just listened:

"'Four score and seven years ago, our fathers brought forth upon this continent a new nation: conceived in liberty, and dedicated to the proposition that all men are created equal.'"

President Lincoln looked excited. “What a wonderful beginning to a speech,” he exclaimed. He moved to the side of the steps. A group of students was gathered around the woman.

“I am proud to see a freed slave instructing a class of students.” President Lincoln smiled for the first time since we met him.

“We’re in the future,” Jacob reminded him. “That teacher isn’t a freed slave. She’s just plain free. Slavery ended after you issued the Emancipation Proclamation.”

“Are you convinced?” Zack asked President Lincoln. “Are you ready to go back to 1862?”

“Hmmm.” Abraham Lincoln studied the teacher a moment. He looked at the kids in the class. “I am beginning to believe that this is indeed another time.”

“‘Now,’” the teacher continued the speech, “‘we are engaged in a great civil war, testing whether that nation, or any nation so conceived and so dedicated, can long endure.’”

Abraham Lincoln’s face turned red. He closed his

eyes and grunted. “I do not need to hear this speech further.” He turned and stomped back down the steps. “If this is the future then nothing has changed. We are still at war.”

“No, no, no. Everything has changed,” I called after him. I hopped down two steps to catch him. He was walking really fast. “Wait! You didn’t even see the giant statue of you.”

“I don’t want to see any statues. The teacher speaks about the Civil War as if it continues,” Abraham Lincoln said without stopping. “If this is the future, then I did nothing. The war still rages. And soldiers still fight.”

“No,” Jacob said, rushing to keep up. “She’s a history teacher, reading your speech.”

“If you’ll go back up, you’ll see,” I added. “Those words are carved on the wall.”

Bo tried to jump ahead of President Lincoln. “She’s reciting the Gettysburg Address. It’s a speech you gave after the battle of Gettysburg in 1863. The war wasn’t over when you spoke, but it was clear to everyone that the North would win.”

"I did not write this speech." Abraham Lincoln walked around Bo. "I have never been to Gettysburg, Pennsylvania."

"Not yet," Jacob said. "But it will be the most famous speech you'll ever give."

"You are mistaken," President Lincoln said as we reached the bottom step. "This is not my speech. And it never will be!"

"We better take him back to 1862," Bo said. "Hopefully a new telegram has come since we've been gone. There is still a little time. Maybe he'll find out the North really did win at Antietam and issue the Emancipation Proclamation."

Jacob took the computer out of his pocket. Our very first mission had failed. What more could go wrong?

Jacob was about to put in the cartridge and send us back to the telegraph office when suddenly a car pulled up to the side of the road.

"Hey, Bob!" a woman shouted through an open window. Abraham Lincoln glanced over at her. His name wasn't Bob, but she was definitely talking to him.

"We've been looking all over for you," she told him. "You're late. Good thing you're already wearing your costume. Let's go."

"Where are we going?" President Lincoln asked.

"The theater, of course," the woman answered. "There's a school group coming to see the play." She opened the car door. "Get in, quick."

"I've always loved the theater." Abraham Lincoln looked at the car. He looked at us and said loudly, "I made no difference to my own time. Everyone wanted me to quit. So I did!" He smiled broadly for the second time that day. "And I am not going back!"

And before Zack could tackle him or Jacob could use the computer or Bo could tell him what he'd read—Abraham Lincoln got into the car and sped away.

We were in big trouble.

Really big trouble.

8

Big Trouble

"What are we going to do?" Zack asked. We watched the car drive away. "I can't believe we lost the president!"

"At least we know he's headed to the theater," Jacob said, looking at the bright side.

"And we know school kids are going to see the show," Bo added.

"And we know that woman thought he was an actor named Bob," I said.

"And she thought he was in costume." Jacob held up four fingers. "That's a lot of clues."

"We've got nothing!" Zack sighed so hard his lips rattled. "We have no idea where he went. Even if we knew which theater, we don't have a car." He pulled his pockets inside out. "And we have no money for a bus."

"Bus!" I said. "That gives me an idea."

The teacher and her students were coming down the memorial steps. I hurried over to her. "Did you come here on a school bus?" I asked.

"Yes," she said slowly, looking at me funny. I guess I should have introduced myself first, but I was anxious to see if I was right. "Are you going to a play today?"

"Yes," she answered. She squinted her eyes at me.

"Is the play about Abraham Lincoln?" I asked.

"Yes," she said. And before she could say anything else, I asked, "Is there an actor named Bob in the show?"

"Wow," she said. "You sure have a lot of questions."

"I'm just curious," I replied. But now I knew these school kids were going to the right theater.

Her school bus was parked near the bottom of the memorial steps. I looked over at the bus. "Can we go with you to the show?"

She thought about it a minute and then said, "I

like curious kids. But where is your teacher?"

"Oh. Umm. They—," I stammered. "He isn't here. We also came with a class group, but got separated. We were in the bathroom. Our class"—I coughed—"is going to the same show." I hated lying, but we really needed a ride. I gave her the world's biggest grin.

"Come on," she said at last. And we climbed on the bus.

We were hot on the president's trail. But when we got to the theater, Bo didn't look good. His face was pale and kind of a pasty green color.

"What's up, Bo?" I asked. "Are you bus sick?"

He didn't speak. He just pointed up at the theater's sign. Jacob read it aloud. "Ford's Theatre." And in case we didn't hear Jacob read it, Zack read the sign again.

Bo swayed as if he were going to faint. "Killed," he mumbled. I shrugged. I had no idea what he was talking about. "Shot," Bo muttered again. Then he said, "Ford's Theatre." And "Balcony."

Jacob was the one who put it all together. "Abraham

Lincoln was assassinated. He was shot during his second term as president by an actor during a play." He looked at Bo. "Are you positive that Abraham Lincoln was killed in the balcony of this theater?"

Bo simply nodded. His knees weakened. He began to sink to the sidewalk.

Jacob grabbed Bo's arm to keep him from falling. "Look," he said, "as much as we might want to, we can't do anything about the fact that he is going to be shot. We aren't supposed to change history. Our job is just to keep it on track."

"I think Jacob's right," I added. "If we try to save him, we'll make a bigger mess of history. The whole world would change."

We all felt sad. We wished we could save his life, but there was no way.

Jacob let go of Bo's arm. Bo began to sink down again.

Zack grabbed him and yanked him up. "Snap out of it." Zack shook Bo's shoulders. "He was killed in his own time, not ours. He's not going to be killed today."

Zack looked at the long line of students shuffling into the playhouse and added, "Unless he's such a bad actor that these kids throw rotten fruit. And hit him in the eye. And he gets a concussion. And his brain begins to bleed. And—"

"We get the point, Zack," Jacob interrupted. He looked at the watch. "We better go. We don't have much time left."

Bo took a deep breath and shook out his legs. He didn't look so green anymore. "Thanks, guys," he said softly.

"Let's focus on getting him to issue the Emancipation Proclamation," I suggested.

And off we went.

We hoped to find Abraham Lincoln before the show started. But we were too late. When we went inside, the theater was dark. The play had already begun.

Abraham Lincoln was standing on the stage. He sat down in a rocking chair under a bright spotlight.

We began to sneak down the aisle toward the front.

"I am Abraham Lincoln," he began. He wasn't

really an actor, so he had a script in his hands. He read: "In my younger days, I did not want to be president."

"Still doesn't," I whispered to Jacob. A lady gave me an evil look and said, "Shh."

I almost blurted out, "Hey, lady, get your money back. This play is going to be over in a minute." But instead, I held my tongue and crept closer to the stage.

Abraham Lincoln held the script up to the light. He was reading very carefully. "I tried to be a store-keeper. My business failed. I wanted to be a farmer. My crops dried up."

Jacob took the computer out of his pocket. We were going to snag him right after he finished reading. We didn't even care that there was a crowd. Hopefully, they'd just think his disappearance was part of the play.

His voice got louder as he continued. "I wanted to be a politician. In 1832, I ran for Legislature. And lost. When I wanted to go to Congress, I lost. I ran for Senate and lost that election too."

Abraham Lincoln stood up and angrily threw the script on the floor. "All I ever wanted to do was to make a difference." He lowered his head. "And I have failed at that, too."

I jumped up on the stage. "No!" I shouted. "You aren't a quitter! There is still time!"

A huge burly man came out of a side curtain. I saw him reach for me. I ducked. He missed me by a mile.

The boys leaped up on the stage. Zack wrapped his arms around President Lincoln's leg. President Lincoln shook his leg and demanded he get off. Zack refused to let go.

People were coming at us from all sides. Security guards came from the wings. Kids jumped up on the stage from the audience. Teachers chased after their students. The stage was crowded with people running around and shouting.

Zack was still hanging on to President Lincoln's leg.

"Hurry," he called to Jacob. "I've got him. Put in the cartridge!"

Jacob surveyed the scene. "No way!" he called back.

"There are too many people." A security guard caught my shirt. I broke free and ran.

"Quiet!" Abraham Lincoln's voice boomed throughout the theater.

I froze. The security guard chasing me froze. No one dared make a sound.

"Thank you," President Lincoln said, his voice strong and determined. He looked down at Zack with piercing eyes. Zack let go of the president's leg.

He turned to me. "Tell me again," he demanded. "What did you say earlier?" I swear if he had laser beams for eyes, I'd be a melted mess.

I took a deep breath and looked him right in the face. "You aren't a quitter!" I answered loudly. My voice echoed in the silent theater.

A little twinkle suddenly gleamed in the president's eye. He bent low and picked the script up off the ground. He read quickly, flipping through the first few pages.

Abraham Lincoln stood up straight. "You are correct. I may have failed many times in my life, but

I have never quit." No one moved as he walked across the stage.

He handed the script back to the woman with the car. "B-but, Bob—," the woman stuttered, "what about the play?"

"I am Abraham Lincoln," he corrected her. "And my country needs me."

Then he turned to Bo, Zack, Jacob, and me. He just looked at us. We didn't need words to understand what he meant. He wanted us to follow him.

Abraham Lincoln led us through the theater and out the front door. "It is time to issue the Emancipation Proclamation and free the slaves," he announced.

"But what about the war?" Zack asked. "Aren't you going to wait for a Northern victory?"

Abraham Lincoln didn't answer right away. He was distracted by something near the roof. He pointed up. Above the theater door was an American flag. He looked puzzled.

"There are fifty stars," Bo said, finding his voice at long last. "One for each state in the union."

"Fifty states," Abraham Lincoln repeated. He shook

his head and grinned. "That reminds me of a joke," he said. "But we don't have time for jokes. I have to free the Southern slaves."

We walked around the back of the building and Jacob slipped the cartridge into the computer. The time-travel hole opened. Glowing green smoke spilled over the pavement.

President Abraham Lincoln jumped in first.

Bo, Jacob, Zack, and I held hands. And followed him home.

9

The Emancipation Proclamation

When we arrived back in 1862, there was one thing on my mind. "How much time is left?" I asked Jacob.

He checked the watch and answered, "Sixteen minutes."

Abraham Lincoln turned to me. "What does 'sixteen minutes' mean?"

"Your cabinet said they would wait for you. But they are leaving in sixteen minutes." I answered.

"You could have told me that earlier!" Abraham Lincoln shouted. He was running toward the White House. I ran after him.

"You wouldn't listen!" I argued.

"You should have made me listen!" Abraham Lincoln

said. He had such long legs, I had to take three steps for every one of his.

We got to the White House in record time. Abraham Lincoln stopped so suddenly, Jacob crashed into his back.

"How can I issue the Emancipation Proclamation and free the Southern slaves without a military victory?" he asked, helping Jacob up. "No one will listen to me."

Bo raised his right hand. "I swear to you the North wins at Antietam. I know it for a fact."

"I trust you," Abraham Lincoln replied. "But how are we going to convince my executive cabinet? William Seward will never believe I went to the future. And he is the one advising me to wait." Abraham Lincoln rubbed his beard.

Bo scratched his chin. "I wonder why the telegram from Antietam hasn't come yet."

I remembered that telegrams have to be issued from a telegraph office. "Maybe there isn't a telegraph office near Antietam," I suggested. "It could have taken a few days for someone to walk to one."

"It has happened before," Abraham Lincoln said, still stroking his beard. "Sometimes the newspapers know about our defeats before I do. Soldiers talk to reporters. Days later, I get the official telegram."

Zack stretched his legs. "Go to the meeting. I'll run to the War Department and check the latest telegrams." He bent low, getting ready.

"He's a good runner," I assured the president. "He's the fastest boy in the whole third grade. He even has a medal to prove it."

"You better hurry," Jacob advised.

"No problem." Zack took off.

We rushed through the entry of the White House and bounded up the stairs. In his office, Abraham Lincoln took the Emancipation Proclamation out of his desk drawer.

Then he said he needed a book. "I cannot read the Emancipation Proclamation without it." He described the cover and told us the book was by Artemis Ward. We didn't understand why it was so important, but if he wasn't going to read the Emancipation Proclamation without it, we were going to help. We rushed around the office, looking for the book.

I found it in a basket under a pile of papers. I didn't look at it. I just handed it to the president. Then Zack ran in. He was out of breath.

"You made it," Jacob said, giving his brother a big slap on the back. "Ten minutes to go."

Zack handed President Lincoln a big stack of telegraph messages.

Abraham Lincoln read through them, dropping each one on the floor as he went. "A defeat," he said, crumpling up a message. "No," he read another. "No. No. No." Three more hit the floor.

And just when we were starting to worry, he found it. "Bully!" he exclaimed, waving a telegram in the air. "We won at Antietam!"

He shook Bo's hand. "You were right. We won five days ago on September seventeenth! The telegraph was delayed." He reread the message. "I am going to have to talk to General McClellan. He made a grave mistake not pursuing the Southern army."

He tucked the telegram in his pocket. "I'll speak to

him tomorrow. Today I am too busy. Today I am going to free the Southern slaves!"

We followed Abraham Lincoln into the executive cabinet room. All the men were gathering their papers, preparing to leave.

"Sit!" Abraham Lincoln commanded. Everyone fell back into chairs. Except us. We stood behind the president.

He took out the book we'd found. It turned out to be a book of jokes. And he read out loud a silly story. I wanted to wave at him, tell him to skip the story. We didn't have time. But President Lincoln loved jokes. And now that he didn't feel sad anymore, he wanted to tell a joke. He was the president and knew what he was doing, so I bit my bottom lip and waited.

And when he was done joking around, President Lincoln did the most important thing he'd ever do: He issued the Emancipation Proclamation.

Afterward, we rushed up to President Lincoln. "You have changed the world," I said.

"You made America great," Zack added.

Bo gave President Lincoln back his coins. "We don't need these," Bo said.

Jacob handed Abraham Lincoln the letter of resignation. "We don't need this, either."

Abraham Lincoln shook hands with each boy. Then he gave me a hug.

"Thank you," he said.

"You're welcome," I replied. And then, before I could stop myself, I said, "You should stay away from Ford's Theatre." I knew I shouldn't say anything, but my heart hurt thinking that this great man was going to be assassinated.

"But I love the theater," Abraham Lincoln said with a puzzled look.

"I hear they have good theater in New York," I replied. "Maybe you could go there instead." He smiled and said he'd think about it. But I knew he'd go to Ford's Theatre on April 14, 1865, and his incredible life would be cut short.

History was back on track. And we had time to spare!

With a minute to go, we left the room and returned

to Abraham Lincoln's office. Jacob pulled the cartridge out of the computer. We were excited to go back to school and tell Mr. C what we had done. And at the same time, we were sorry to say good-bye. It had been a great adventure.

The green hole opened in the floor next to the president's desk. Jacob and Zack jumped in first.

As the hole was closing, Bo turned his head to take one last look at the men from his books.

"He's writing it down, you know," he said to me. We held hands, ready to jump.

"Writing what?" I asked. I turned my head to look where Bo was looking. Through the open door, I could see Abraham Lincoln sitting at the long meeting table. While the men chattered around him, he was writing on the back of an envelope.

The same envelope that held his letter of resignation.

"What is he writing?" I asked Bo. The hole was shrinking. The green fog was getting thinner.

"The beginning of the Gettysburg Address," he answered.

"Should we stop him?" I asked. "Abraham Lincoln really shouldn't be writing the Gettysburg Address before the battle of Gettysburg, should he?"

Bo just shrugged.

And together we jumped.

10

Home Again

"Two hours, zero seconds," Jacob announced. We were back at school. We landed outside near the picnic tables.

"We did it!" Bo did a little happy dance. I joined Bo in the dance.

Zack gave high fives to everyone. "I knew we could do it!" he cheered.

"I thought you wanted to get a dog instead," I said.

"I never said that." Zack winked. "I'm allergic to dogs."

We all laughed.

We had done it. We had fixed history by convincing Abraham Lincoln not to quit.

"Let's go tell Mr. Caruthers," Jacob suggested.

Bo, Zack, and I followed Jacob into the building and down the hall. The door to Mr. Caruthers's classroom was open.

"We're back," Jacob told him.

Mr. Caruthers was sitting at his desk. He was grading papers. He took off his glasses.

"So you are," he said slowly. "Shall we see how you did?"

"We—," Bo began.

Mr. Caruthers put a finger over his lips. "Shh. Don't tell me."

"Come here, Abigail." Mr. Caruthers moved to the side. He handed me a big book. I read the title out loud: *"The People Who Shaped America."*

"Turn to page 104," he told me.

I flipped through the pages. There it was: a painting of Abraham Lincoln. He was sitting at a small table. Seven men were sitting near him. I immediately recognized William Seward and Edwin Stanton. "This is a picture of President Lincoln's executive cabinet," I said proudly.

"Yes, it is," Mr. C confirmed. "Read the caption,

Abigail." Mr. Caruthers pointed to the words below the picture.

"'*The First Reading of the Emancipation Proclamation Before the Cabinet*,'" I read. "'An engraving based on the 1864 painting by Francis Bicknell Carpenter.'" I looked down at the picture and felt really good.

"You saved history," Mr. Caruthers said. I could tell he was very proud of us.

I couldn't stop smiling. I saw my paper sitting on Mr. Caruthers's desk. I thought about what I'd written. What if we hadn't been able to convince him? What if Abraham Lincoln quit and never issued the Emancipation Proclamation?

Luckily, we'd never know.

Jacob handed Mr. Caruthers the computer and cartridge.

"Mr. Caruthers?" There was something I needed to know. "You said that each of us has a special skill." I took a deep breath and bravely continued. "Jacob is great with computers. Zack can run really fast. Bo loves to read. But what about me? Why am I part of the team?"

Mr. C simply grinned. "We need you, Abigail," he said, "because you are curious." I couldn't help but smile.

"Well, then, I do have a few questions," I said with a laugh. "In fact, I think we all have some questions."

We all started talking at the same time.

"Where did the computer come from?" I asked.

"Where did you get the cartridge?" Bo interrupted me.

"What would have happened if we ran out of time?" I interrupted Bo.

"How did you know Abraham Lincoln quit?" Zack interrupted me.

"Have all your 'what if' questions been true?" Jacob interrupted Zack.

I interrupted everyone. "Do you only time-travel on Mondays?" Then, before anyone else could speak, I asked another one. "Is that why your clothes are always messy on Mondays?" And another. "Why aren't our clothes messy too?"

Mr. C began to laugh. He leaned back in his chair and folded his arms behind his head. "You don't need to know everything today," he said with a wink. "Your questions will all be answered in good time." He laughed a little harder. "Besides," he said, "it's time for you kids to go home. I know for a fact that you have homework."

"Look," Zack said suddenly, pointing out the classroom window. "Isn't that Mom's van?"

Jacob squinted past Mr. Caruthers. "Yeah. What is she doing here? She's early. She isn't supposed to come until—" Jacob looked at the watch. "It's five minutes after five o'clock."

"We're five minutes late!" Zack said, smacking his forehead.

"Did we lose five minutes somewhere?" I asked, thinking about how Mr. C was late to class every Monday. "Is that another one of the computer's glitches?"

Mr. Caruthers put his glasses back on. "Nah." He shook his head and laughed a little. "I'm late on Mondays because I can never seem to find my car keys in the morning." Then he added in a whisper, "I always work late on Sunday night."

"What are you working on?" I asked the question so quickly all my words sounded like one big long one.

He winked, but didn't answer. "Anyway, I always forget to leave my keys where I can find them. And so I'm late to class." Then he raised his eyebrows and said, "Seems you kids are running late today too."

"Well, that's the answer to one of our questions." Zack held up one finger. "That only leaves a hundred more to go." He laughed.

Jacob took off Mr. Caruthers's watch and handed it back to him. "Our mom's waiting. We better get out of here."

"Keep the watch," Mr. Caruthers said. "And keep this, too." Mr. Caruthers handed Jacob the computer. He tucked the cartridge in his drawer.

There was a funny twinkle in Mr. C's eye. "Let's meet in the gym after school next Monday," he said.

I was really excited. "You bet," I said. Bo, Zack, and Jacob agreed.

Jacob handed me the computer. "Your sister is older. She doesn't play with your stuff," Jacob said. "Our baby brother might break it if he finds it in my room."

Very carefully, I put the computer into my backpack.

We said good-bye to Mr. Caruthers. Then we hurried outside together.

"This is the beginning of a terrific adventure," Bo shouted as he went to get his bike.

I was all set to walk home when Jacob asked if I wanted a ride. "Sure," I answered.

"You're late," Mrs. Osborn said after she opened the door for us. "I was getting worried."

"Sorry, Mom," Jacob and Zack said together. "We lost track of time."

"Sorry, Mrs. Osborn," I added as we climbed into the van. "Thanks for driving me home."

Baby Gabe was in his car seat. I gave him a kiss on his head. Jacob and Zack had the cutest brother. But they were right; he would break the computer if we kept it at their house.

"What did you do after school today?" Mrs. Osborn asked.

"We joined a new history club," Jacob answered.

I waved to Bo as he sped off on his bike. I had a strong feeling that when Mr. C sent Bo to get his backpack, it was on purpose.

"Did you have a good time?" Mrs. Osborn asked.

"It was a blast." Zack smiled.

I held my backpack close and said, "A blast to the past."

Emancipation Proclamation

By the president of the United States of America:

A Proclamation

Whereas on the 22nd day of September, A.D. 1862, a proclamation was issued by the president of the United States, containing, among other things, the following, to wit:

"That on the 1st day of January, A.D. 1863, all persons held as slaves within any State or designated part of a State the people whereof shall then be in rebellion against the United States shall be then, thenceforward, and forever free; and the executive government of the United States, including the military and naval authority thereof, will recognize and maintain the freedom of such persons and will do no act or acts to repress such persons, or any of them, in any efforts they may make for their actual freedom.

"That the executive will on the 1st day of January

aforesaid, by proclamation, designate the States and parts of States, if any, in which the people thereof, respectively, shall then be in rebellion against the United States; and the fact that any State or the people thereof shall on that day be in good faith represented in the Congress of the United States by members chosen thereto at elections wherein a majority of the qualified voters of such States shall have participated shall, in the absence of strong countervailing testimony, be deemed conclusive evidence that such State and the people thereof are not then in rebellion against the United States."

Now, therefore, I, Abraham Lincoln, president of the United States, by virtue of the power in me vested as Commander-in-Chief of the Army and Navy of the United States in time of actual armed rebellion against the authority and government of the United States, and as a fit and necessary war measure for supressing said rebellion, do, on this 1st day of January, A.D. 1863, and in accordance with my purpose so to do, publicly proclaimed for the full period of one hundred days from the first day above mentioned, order and designate as the States and parts of States wherein the people thereof, respectively, are this day in rebellion against the United States the following, to wit:

Arkansas, Texas, Louisiana (except the parishes of St. Bernard, Palquemines, Jefferson, St. John, St. Charles, St. James, Ascension, Assumption, Terrebone, Lafourche, St. Mary, St. Martin, and Orleans, including the city of New Orleans), Mississippi, Alabama, Florida, Georgia, South Carolina, North Carolina, and Virginia (except the forty-eight counties designated as West Virginia, and also the counties of Berkeley, Accomac, Morthhampton, Elizabeth City, York, Princess Anne, and Norfolk, including the cities of Norfolk and Portsmouth), and which excepted parts are for the present left precisely as if this proclamation were not issued.

And by virtue of the power and for the purpose aforesaid, I do order and declare that all persons held as slaves within said designated States and parts of States are, and henceforward shall be, free; and that the Executive Government of the United States, including the military and naval authorities thereof, will recognize and maintain the freedom of said persons.

And I hereby enjoin upon the people so declared to be free to abstain from all violence, unless in necessary self-defence; and I recommend to them that, in all case when allowed, they labor faithfully for reasonable wages.

And I further declare and make known that such persons of suitable condition will be received into the armed service of the United States to garrison forts, positions, stations, and other places, and to man vessels of all sorts in said service.

And upon this act, sincerely believed to be an act of justice, warranted by the Constitution upon military necessity, I invoke the considerate judgment of mankind and the gracious favor of Almighty God.

Gettysburg Address

Four score and seven years ago, our fathers brought forth upon this continent a new nation: conceived in liberty, and dedicated to the proposition that all men are created equal.

Now we are engaged in a great civil war . . . testing whether that nation, or any nation so conceived and so dedicated . . . can long endure. We are met on a great battlefield of that war.

We have come to dedicate a portion of that field as a final resting place for those who here gave their lives that that nation might live. It is altogether fitting and proper that we should do this.

But, in a larger sense, we cannot dedicate . . . we cannot consecrate . . . we cannot hallow this ground. The brave men, living and dead, who struggled here have consecrated it, far above our poor power to add or detract. The world will little note, nor long remember, what we say here, but it can never forget what they did here.

It is for us the living, rather, to be dedicated here to the unfinished work which they who fought here have thus far so nobly advanced. It is rather for us to be here dedicated to the great task remaining before us . . . that from these honored dead we take increased devotion to that cause for which they gave the last full measure of devotion . . . that we here highly resolve that these dead shall not have died in vain . . . that this nation, under God, shall have a new birth of freedom . . . and that government of the people . . . by the people . . . for the people . . . shall not perish from the earth.

Delivered on November 19, 1863, at the dedication of the national cemetery on the Civil War battlefield, Gettysburg, Pennsylvania. This is the Hay version of the Gettysburg Address, which is held in the Library of Congress Manuscript Division.

A Letter to Our Readers

Hi! We hope you enjoyed *Lincoln's Legacy*.

The story we have told about Abraham Lincoln is part fact, part fiction. Time travel is fiction. We made that up because it is fun and exciting. But the things the kids see, both in the past and in the present—those things are real.

In 1862, cows ran through the streets of Washington almost every day. They were brought to feed the soldiers. Hot air balloons left the city to spy on the South. There were army parades. And since few streets were paved, the city was messy and dirty.

The White House was exactly as we described. And the men who aided President Lincoln—they were all real too. When the president's secretary says that the White House basement smelled like a swamp, that was also real.

As far as we know, Abraham Lincoln was never really going to quit. But all the reasons we told you that he might have quit are true. The Southern states left the Union because he was elected, the newspapers called him mean names, and many of his top advisers wanted him to quit.

And though Abraham Lincoln did love telling jokes, he wasn't always a happy man. Sometimes he put his head down and felt bad. And sadly, President Lincoln really was assassinated in the balcony of Ford's Theatre while watching a play.

If you look at the back of a penny, you'll find a picture of the Lincoln Memorial. This building, in Washington, D.C., reminds us that President Lincoln was a great man. He changed our world when he issued the Emancipation Proclamation. He freed the Southern slaves and helped shape America into the great country it is today.

If you want to learn more about the Blast to the Past series, or want to contact us, visit our website at BlastToThePastBooks.com.

Enjoy!
Stacia and Rhody

BLAST TO THE PAST

in the next adventure:

#2 *Disney's Dream*

The car screeched to a stop in front of West Hudson Elementary School.

"Hurry up, Abigail," my sister commanded. "You're going to be late to meet your teacher."

I checked the dashboard clock. I had plenty of time. CeCe just wanted to get rid of me.

I leaned over to tie my shoe. Not because it needed to be tied, but just to bug her.

I peeked in my backpack to make sure that the time-travel computer was hidden safely inside. I looked inside my homework folder. Then I took out my coin purse and counted my money. I put the coin purse back and finally zipped up my backpack. After all that, I slowly opened the car door and stepped out onto the sidewalk.

The instant I closed the door, CeCe sped off, leaving a cloud of dust behind her.

I was brushing off my pants when my friend Bo came up beside me.

Bo's real name is Roberto. He's the new kid at school.

"Hey, Abigail!" Bo pointed at the car. We heard the tires squeal as CeCe left the parking lot. "What's your sister's rush?"

"CeCe got her driver's license this year," I answered. "Mom lets her drive the car because she works at a movie theater after school." I slung my backpack over one shoulder.

"Oh, yeah. I see her there all the time. The Happy Times Movie Theater," Bo said, tipping his own backpack onto its wheels. "I like that place. On Mondays, they charge nineteen-twenties prices."

"Yeah. Well, Mom said since CeCe has the car today, she had to drop me off early this morning. There is nothing CeCe hates more than driving me places."

"Does she always zoom off like that?" Bo asked. He was talking pretty loudly—for Bo. He used to be so shy and quiet that I could barely hear him. But ever since we'd time-traveled together, he'd gotten a little louder. Or else I'd developed supersonic hearing.

"Yep. She wants to get away from me as fast as she can." I thought about all the other times she'd rushed me out of the car. "We don't get along. In fact, she tattles on me all the time. She's always trying to get me in trouble." Sometimes I think Bo is really lucky to be an only child.

"What do you do about it?" Bo asked.

"I work extra hard to make her crazy. I tell on her too. We're in a big war." I smiled mischievously. "I can be really annoying when I want to be."

"You definitely annoyed her today," Bo said, and laughed a little laugh. Then he said, "Don't you think it's weird that Mr. C wants us to meet him in the gym before school? I mean, I'm never up this early."

Mr. Caruthers is our third-grade teacher. He's so cool, we call him "Mr. C."

"Yeah," I agreed. "It's weird. I thought I was in

trouble when he called me at home yesterday. Then I found out he called the twins, too."

We headed around the back of the school building.

"Mr. C told my mom we were going to have a special History Club meeting this morning," Bo said with a wink.

We knew what "History Club" meant. It's what we like to call our time-traveling adventures.

Of course, we'd only had one History Club meeting so far.

I patted the outside of my backpack, thinking about the time-travel computer inside.

Last Monday, Mr. C had given us the computer. When we put a special cartridge into its back, a glowing green hole opened up in the floor. We jumped in. And that's how we traveled through time. Taking the cartridge out brought us home again.

When he first handed us the computer and cartridge, Mr. C explained that, for some reason, famous Americans from the past were giving up their dreams. They weren't inventing, speaking out, or fighting for what was right. They were quitting!

A sticker on each cartridge showed us who we were going to visit. Our mission was to make sure that the person didn't quit! The tricky part was that we only had two hours to get the job done.

Our first mission had been a total success. We visited Abraham Lincoln in 1862 and convinced him to issue the Emancipation Proclamation, which he did—on September 22, 1862.

I pulled my backpack closer and made a wish: "I hope this History Club meeting means we get to time-travel again today," I whispered so softly, no one could hear me.

Then, in my normal voice, I asked Bo, "Where do you think the twins are?" Jacob and Zack were in our class and lived next door to me.

Bo shrugged. "Maybe they're already inside," he said.

Someone had propped the gym door open. We let ourselves in.

Jacob and Zack were waiting for us by the basketball hoop. When I saw them, I started to giggle. Soon I was laughing so hard that my eyes filled with tears.

Jacob and Zack were wearing red-and-purple-striped sweatpants with matching hooded jackets. I see Jacob and Zack every day at school and on weekends, too. The twins hadn't dressed alike since kindergarten. They looked ridiculous.

Jacob gave me a mean look. "Stop it!" he demanded. "Grandma sent us new clothes." He sighed a big sigh. It was the kind of sigh you make when you really have no choice.

"Mom said we had to wear them," Zack added, tugging at the zipper on his jacket. It was jammed. "I think I'm going to be stuck wearing this forever," he moaned.

At that moment, Mr. Caruthers walked into the gym.

"Hey! Look at Mr. C!" I pointed at our teacher.

Mr. C was wearing a suit and a bow tie. His hair was neatly combed. His shirt was tucked into his pants. Even his glasses were sitting nicely on his nose.

"What's the deal?" Zack asked in surprise. "He's usually a wreck on Mondays."

When Mr. C came to class on Monday mornings,

his suit was *always* crumpled, his hair *always* stuck up, and his glasses were *always* crooked.

"Hmmm," Bo muttered, scratching his chin. He does that when he's thinking really hard. "Something weird is going on."

"I'm glad you all could make it," Mr. Caruthers said to us. "Follow me." We walked across the gym to the back stairs. "This way." Mr. C disappeared down the stairs. "Are you coming?" he called up to us.

I had never seen anyone go near the steps at the back of the gym. It was dark down there. If a basketball bounced down those steps, there was not one kid in the whole school brave enough to go get it.

By the look on Bo's face, I knew he wasn't going to be the first to go down the stairs. Not because the basement was creepy, but because Mr. Caruthers was down there. Bo might talk a little louder to us kids, but he was still really nervous around adults.

I was curious. But not curious enough to go down to the super-scary basement.

We all stood around, silently staring at the stairwell.

Finally, Jacob moved forward and said, "If I can

jump into a green glowing hole and time-travel, I can walk down the gym stairs." Jacob is always ready for an adventure.

"If I can wear this stupid sweat suit in public," Zack said, "I can definitely go into the basement." He followed Jacob. I was surprised because Zack is never very brave.

Once there were other kids in the basement, Bo was willing to go. "Come on, Abigail. We have to go if we want to time-travel again," Bo said as he disappeared into the darkness.

"Okay," I told myself, "the faster I go down, the sooner I can come back up."

My heart was racing as I jumped onto the first step.

NANCY DREW AND THE CLUE CREW®

Test your detective skills with more Clue Crew cases!

#1 *Sleepover Sleuths*
#2 *Scream for Ice Cream*
#3 *Pony Problems*
#4 *The Cinderella Ballet Mystery*
#5 *Case of the Sneaky Snowman*
#6 *The Fashion Disaster*
#7 *The Circus Scare*
#8 *Lights, Camera . . . Cats!*
#9 *The Halloween Hoax*
#10 *Ticket Trouble*
#11 *Ski School Sneak*
#12 *Valentine's Day Secret*
#13 *Chick-napped!*
#14 *The Zoo Crew*
#15 *Mall Madness*
#16 *Thanksgiving Thief*
#17 *Wedding Day Disaster*
#18 *Earth Day Escapade*
#19 *April Fool's Day*
#20 *Treasure Trouble*
#21 *Double Take*
#22 *Unicorn Uproar*
#23 *Babysitting Bandit*
#24 *Princess Mix-up Mystery*
#25 *Buggy Breakout*
#26 *Camp Creepy*
#27 *Cat Burglar Caper*
#28 *Time Thief*
#29 *Designed for Disaster*
#30 *Dance Off*
#31 *The Make-a-Pet Mystery*
#32 *Cape Mermaid Mystery*
#33 *The Pumpkin Patch Puzzle*
#34 *Cupcake Chaos*
#35 *Cooking Camp Disaster*
#36 *The Secret of the Scarecrow*

FROM ALADDIN • PUBLISHED BY SIMON & SCHUSTER

SECRET FILES

HARDY BOYS®

Follow the trail with Frank and Joe Hardy in this chapter book mystery series!

#1 Trouble at the Arcade
#2 The Missing Mitt
#3 Mystery Map
#4 Hopping Mad
#5 A Monster of a Mystery
#6 The Bicycle Thief
#7 The Disappearing Dog
#8 Sports Sabotage
#9 The Great Coaster Caper
#10 A Rockin' Mystery
#11 Robot Rumble
#12 Lights, Camera . . . Zombies!
#13 Balloon Blow-Up

BY FRANKLIN W. DIXON

FROM ALADDIN • EBOOK EDITIONS ALSO AVAILABLE
KIDS.SIMONANDSCHUSTER.COM

Join Zeus and his friends as they set off on the adventure of a lifetime.

EBOOK EDITIONS ALSO AVAILABLE

From Aladdin • KIDS.SimonandSchuster.com